Called as Crazy, Eccentric & Psychotic Turned into

Great Scientists

Krishna Murty Kommmajosyula

Here's to the crazy ones, the misfits, the rebels, the troublemakers, the round pegs in the square holes... the ones who see things differently – they're not fond of rules... You can quote them, disagree with them, glorify or vilify them, but the only thing you can't do is ignore them because they change things... they push the human race forward and while some may see them as the crazy ones, we see genius, because the ones who are crazy enough to think that they can change the world, are the ones who do.

– Steve Jobs

Publishers

Pustak Mahal®

Administrative office and sale centre

J-3/16, Daryaganj, New Delhi-110002

☎ 23276539, 23272783, 23272784 • *Fax:* 011-23260518

E-mail: info@pustakmahal.com • *Website:* www.pustakmahal.com

Branches

Bengaluru: ☎ 080-22234025 • *Telefax:* 080-22240209

E-mail: pustakmahalblr@gmail.com

Mumbai: ☎ 022-22010941, 022-22053387

E-mail: unicornbooksmumbai@gmail.com

ISBN 978-81-223-1286-7

Edition: 2018

Printed at: Param Offsetters, Okhla, Delhi

DEDICATION

TO MY UNCLE WHO SHAPED MY LIFE

Sri K. G. Rao B. A.

Expert in Rubber Plantation (Malaya, Indonesia, Sri Lanka, India)

PREFACE

Whenever I go to book stalls, I see them lined with so-called motivational books and management books enlightening us to do this or that, taking cues from the winning sportsman, successful businessman and practical politicians.

But there would be no better inspirational examples than from the lives of the scientists. They bring us fascinating stories of their trials and tribulations; struggles and challenges; dreams and delusions; endeavours and achievements. Those mesmerizing inventions have certainly altered the course of human history. But I am fascinated by their lives which leave indelible impressions of live models for us to emulate. They stir our intellect, instruct, inspire, and invigorate our lives. Real life that educates and entertains! Why not shape our lives with those scientists? These real life sculptures can manage and motivate our lives into better worldliness.

Picking those flowers of emotional intelligence, professional perseverance, disability to be defeated, I wove a colourful garland. But I started showing those flowers or my articles to Mr. Aditya Bhaskaran and Ms. Anusha Mandavilli, then my engineer trainees, who made youthful embellishments.

Contents

★★

I know that I have never invented anything. I have been a medium by which these things were given to the culture as fast as the culture could earn them. I give all the credit to God."

Farnsworth called his device the "Image Dissector." As the name suggests it would transmit an image by dissecting it into individual elements and convert the elements – one line at a time – into an electrical wave, 'scanning' in the present-day term.

A year had gone by. The first few tests revealed very little, nothing except electronic interference on the cathode ray tube. Not in the least discouraged, he improved his system continuously. September 7th 1927 was the fateful day. He painted a thick straight line onto a glass slide and placed in front of the camera. Think of the wondrous delight of all those present in the other room when they could see the straight-line image gleaming boldly in the electronic background on the bottom of Farnsworth's magic tubes. When the slide was rotated, the image on the receiver rotated as well! The first time the transmission of visual intelligence electronically from one place to another. The very first time!

Boy's Battle

But that was the beginning of a boy's classic struggle. Fire swept through the second floor of 202 Green Street where all the experiments were made, burning every piece equipment, labouriously built by Philo. Natural disasters could not fail Farnsworth, but human nature could, well almost! Radio Corporation of America had interests in everything in electronics those days, virtually ruled the waves. David Sarnoff, the recently appointed Vice-President and General Manager of the vast Radio Corporation of America wasn't taking any chances. He would not like to let go the new fad out of his hands. His famous quote: "The RCA doesn't pay patent royalties, we collect them." So television, if ever had to be under his control.

When his researches did not yield fruitful results, Sarnoff even engaged prowlers around 202 Green Street, Farnsworth's lab, the only television address. Vladimir K. Zworykin was developing television on behalf of RCA. When he saw Fansworth's TV, Zworykin said, "This is a beautiful instrument. I wish I'd invented it." RCA pressed into service some of the best legal brains and charged their biggest legal guns to fight Philo on the patent of television. It was then when his old chemistry teacher also came and testified.

RCA Pays

Add to these troubles which kept him away from his active research, his second son died. But justice was delayed but not denied: "Priority of invention is awarded to Philo T. Farnsworth." RCA had to shell down royalty for patent license for the first time to an independent inventor.

Thousands lined up to see the new electronic marvel at the first public demonstration of Farnsworth TV at Philadelphia's Franklin Institute. When the man landed on moon, entire planet was watching that "one small step for mankind" on their television sets; he turned to his wife and said: "This has made it all worthwhile." One small step for mankind! One small imagination of farm boy of scanning the image! It is still the only method of moving picture transmission electronically!

He depended on his imagination, maintained his independence of thought and action, nourished his original thinking, and worked with his intelligence and added his experience. This does not mean that you must come up with radical ideas, every time you come across a simple problem. Fine if you can get even a simpler solution to a simple problem.

Final Irony

Finally, here is the irony! When he appeared in 1957 on a popular TV quiz show, "I've Got a Secret," nobody recognized him. He was identified only as "Dr. X". Audience was asked to identify him with some clues. One of the celebrity panelists Bill Cullen asked if he had invented some kind of machine that might be painful when used. The mysterious doctor replied, "Yes, sometimes, it's most painful."

Revealing his identity as the father of electronic television, the final word on Philo came from Program anchor: "We'd all be out of work if it weren't for you."

In the beginning, there was only an imagination; in the middle there was struggle, struggle making his imagination work and struggle with the giants who wanted to snatch the very fruits of his imagination. In the end, oblivion! That's Philo T. Farnsworth!!!

> ***Here's to the crazy ones, the misfits, the rebels, the troublemakers, the round pegs in the square holes... the ones who see things differently – they're not fond of rules... You can quote them, disagree with them, glorify or vilify them, but the only thing you can't do is ignore them because they change things... they push the human race forward, and while some may see them as the crazy ones, we see genius, because the ones who are crazy enough to think that they can change the world, are the ones who do.***
>
> ***– Steve Jobs***

LEARN FROM NATURE

Charles F. Kettering was a holder or co-holder of more than 300 patents as wide ranging as the auto starter for automobiles, leaded gasoline (lead as anti-knock agent), the motorization of the cash register, portable lighting generator, Freon refrigerant, automobile paint, an incubator for premature babies, and even a treatment for venereal disease. He received many honorary doctorates and degrees plus dozens of other citations and medals.

Charles F. Kettering

He says, "When a scientist conquers something, he abides by the fundamental laws and does so with Nature's permission. He has learned that conquering is submission." Submit yourself to the nature and learn more and more secrets. Great Sea of truth lay all undiscovered before you. But Louis Agassiz warned, "The study of Nature is intercourse with the Highest Mind. You should never trifle with Nature."

The velcro fastener was invented in 1941 by George de Mestral, a Swiss engineer. One day after returning from a walk through Alps, he observed some burs that kept sticking to his clothes and dog's fur. He took a closer look and even examined the burs under a microscope. He decided to copy the unique fastener mechanism, the natural microscopic hooks. As usual, people laughed at him. But he kept on and by trial and error he came up with his final product. Using nylon and infra red light he developed tiny and tough hooks. Mestral named his invention Velcro after the French words "velours" (meaning velvet) and "crochet" (hook)? De Mestral once offered an advice to Velcro executives: "If any of your employees ask for a two-week holiday to go hunting, say yes." He knows the fruits.

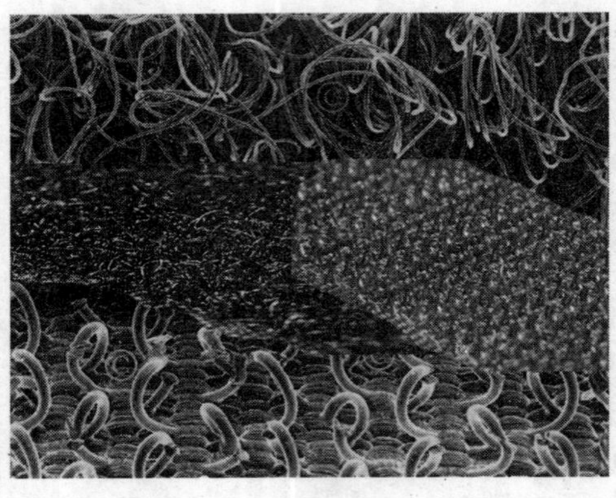

Velcro fastener

Chance does not make discoveries, prepared mind makes them. Speaking at the inauguration of the Faculty of Science at the University of Lille in 1854, the French scientist Louis Pasteur made a statement which is as relevant today as it was then: "In the field of observation, chance favours only the prepared mind."

The scientist or the researcher must walk with a prepared mind, through the Nature's mysterious ways. Catch an unforeseen incident or occurrence and understand it. Use it constructively. Do not overlook an unexpected chance event. Science education fosters your mind and makes it critical, informed and open mind to deliver tomorrow's innovations. Are you tempted? Open your senses and mind! One day you may run crying "Eureka"! Don't do that naked!!!

Seeds were sown on the sea-shore of Rameswaram. Inspiration from a teacher became a mission of life and a full time passion for a village lad who later presided over this country. A simple teacher from a village school showed the way, nature's way.

This is from the story of Abdul Kalam, who needs no introduction. Highly respected and truly Gandhian, Shri Sivasubramaniya Iyer was his primary school teacher.

Let us learn the story in Kalam's words.

"One day he was teaching about bird's flight. He drew a diagram of a bird on the blackboard depicting the wings, tail and the body structure with the head. He explained how the birds create the lift and fly, and how they change direction while flying. At the end of the class, he wanted to know whether we understood how the birds fly. I said, "I did not understand how the birds fly." When I said this, the teacher asked the other students whether they understood or not. Many students said that they also did not understand. He did not get upset by our response since he was a committed teacher. Our teacher said that he would take all of us to the sea shore.

That evening the whole class was at the sea shore of Rameswaram. We enjoyed the roaring sea waves knocking at the sandy hills in the pleasant evening. Birds were flying with sweet chirping voice. He showed the sea birds in formations of 10 to 20 numbers. We saw the marvelous formations of birds with a purpose and we were all amazed. He showed us the birds and asked us to see that when the birds fly, what they looked like. We saw the wings flapping. He asked us to look at the tail portion with the combination of flapping wings and twisting tail. We noticed closely and found that the birds in that condition flew in the direction they desired.

Then he asked us a question, where the engine is and how it is powered. Bird is powered by its own life and the motivation of what it wants. All these things were explained to us within fifteen minutes. We all understood the whole bird dynamics from this practical example. How nice it was? Our teacher was a great teacher; he could give us a theoretical lesson coupled with a live practical example available in nature. This is real teaching.

Again quoting Kalam,

"For me, it was not merely an understanding of how a bird flies. The bird's flight entered into me and created a special feeling. The event that I witnessed decided my future career. When I went to engineering in Madras Institute of Technology, I took Aeronautical Engineering."

Rest is history. After all, Joseph Fourier said, "The profound study of nature is the most fertile source of mathematical discoveries."

We feel enchanted with the present day electronic marvels. 'Man has attempted to duplicate some of the feats of the animal world and in recent years science has given us instrumentation that has done very well indeed.' (Kettering) The modern marvels are intertwined in our lives so very badly that we cannot imagine a witch removing them from our lives with a wand.

Sound echo devices which bat has been using for its travel in the dark for thousands of years are much more sophisticated than our systems. We wonder at the autopilot of planes and instrument landing systems but every year flocks of birds fly thousands of kilometres across vast lands and seas to new places and return to precisely their native location. Their instrumentation is natural and phenomenal but only very little was understood by us.

Nature teaches more than she preaches. There are no sermons in stones. "It is easier to get a spark out of a stone than a moral", says John Burroughs. We talk about conquering nature. But we are a long way.

Very humbly, Isaac Newton says, "I was like a boy playing on the sea-shore, and diverting myself now and then finding a smoother pebble or a prettier shell than ordinary, whilst the great ocean of truth lay all undiscovered before me."

We have learnt from our school days that Newton invented his theories of gravitation when an apple fell on his head. Did the apple go into his brain and created a brainstorming session with the result that he discovered the laws? Nature finds ingenious ways to reveal itself.

Many of us must have seen apples or mangoes falling but none of us bother to find the reason. Why? Rain drops fall and snowflakes drop. We enjoy them. But Newton was working hard on complex geometrical and mathematical problems and could not find a solution. He took a break and started taking rest under the shade of an apple tree, when the revelation by way of an apple came near him. Just then it occurred to him that a force of nature pulled the apple to the ground instead of the tree throwing it down. Nature triggered his many years of study into discovery of properties of physical science and physical laws.

Learning is not compulsory... neither is survival.

– W. Edwards Deming

I Can Make It

One day in the late nineteenth century a certain Bishop Wright was discussing science with a college professor. The bishop felt that everything about nature had already been discovered.

The professor politely told the bishop that he was mistaken. "The scientists would invent even more in the near future," he felt, "why, in a few years we'll be able to fly through the air."

"Nonsense!" Bishop Wright said, "Flight is for the birds and the angels."

He had every reason to say so. From times immemorial, man tried to fly like a bird and every one of them failed, failed miserably. Even more recently...

Samuel Langley

Progress in Flying Machines

Samuel Langley was physicist and astronomer who conducted experiments with flying machines. He had been interested in flight, "...as long as I can remember anything."

Samuel Langley received a $70,000 grant. Langley gave up the project after two crashes on October 7 and December 8, 1903.

Sir George Cayley is known as the father of aerodynamics. Cayley wrote an article "On Ariel Navigation" that showed a fixed wing aircraft with powered propulsion and a tail for controlling the aeroplane. He felt that it would be the best way for man to fly.

German engineer, Otto Lilienthal was the first person to design a glider that could fly a person and was able to fly long distances. Basing his studies on flying birds, he wrote a book on aerodynamics in 1889. After more than 2500 flights with his machine, in one ill- fated flight he lost control because of a sudden strong wind. It crashed into the ground, killing him instantly.

Aeroplanes were a hobby for Octave Chanute, a successful engineer. Inspired by Otto Lilienthal, Chanute designed his most successful the Herring - Chanute biplane. With all the information he could gather, Chanute published "Progress in Flying Machines" in 1894.

Though they had the passion to fly, they could not make it happen. To top it, everyone around, including great men discouraged these fancy ideas. Ferdinand Foch, a Professor of Strategy said, "Aeroplanes are interesting toys but of no military value."

Going back to the top story, Bishop Wright was the father of two young budding inventors named Orville and Wilbur!

Fascination for Birds

The Wright brothers were fascinated by the birds and studied their every detail. They wanted to fly. But they knew every one of them who tried earlier has failed. Senior Wright was not convinced that man can ever fly. Yet they thought they can fly. They read every piece of material available those days. They studied the works of Otto Lilienthal. Chanute's "Progress in Flying Machines" became the basis of their experiments. They were in contact with Chanute and often sought his advice.

Lord Kelvin is one of those most respected scientists after whom a measurement of temperature is named. He thought and said in no uncertain terms that "Heavier-than-air flying machines are impossible."

Wilbur Wright

But that did not deter Wilbur and his brother Orville from designing a series of gliders and flying them as both unmanned (as kites) and piloted flights. They had hoped that they can do it. Wilbur Wright said, "I am an enthusiast, but not a crank in the sense that I have some pet theories as to the proper construction of a flying machine. I wish to avail myself of all that is already known and then, if possible, add my mite to help on the future worker who will attain final success."

In 1900, the Wrights successfully tested their new 50-pound biplane glider with its 17-foot wingspan and wing-warping mechanism at Kitty Hawk, in both unmanned and piloted flights. In fact, it was the first piloted glider.

I can Do It!

Even after this success, Wilber started entertaining doubts of their experiments. On the advice and Weather Bureau reports, they decided to go to Kitty Hawk, North Carolina, for their first experiments. They had series of unsuccessful days of testing their latest glider at Kitty Hawk, and they were crestfallen by the results. On Aug. 11, 1901, Wright Brothers were riding a train home to Dayton, Ohio, Wilbur said, "Not within a thousand years will man ever fly."

First flight of the Wright Flyer I, December 17, 1903, Orville piloting, Wilbur running at wingtip.

But Orville was confident, "I can do it!"

They dived into their passion more deeply. "It is possible to fly

air lift and turned by warping, or changing the shape of a portion of the wing. Why not try?

Langley was also trying his best to beat the skies. On October 7th 1903, Langley launched a huge 54-foot-long flying machine from a catapult on the Potomac River. While the cameras turned to record the moment, it fell into the river. On December 8th he tried again. This time the rear wing caved in before it got off its catapult. His assistant was luckily saved. Congress criticized him for his waste of money. As usual New York Times Editorial on December 10, 1903 questioned the wisdom of Langley on heavier than air machines.

"...We hope that Professor Langley will not put his substantial greatness as a scientist in further peril by continuing to waste his time and the money involved, in further airship experiments. Life is short, and he is capable of services to humanity incomparably greater than can be expected to result from trying to fly....For students and investigators of the Langley type there are more useful employments."

But exactly seven days later, it happened that on December 17, 1903, after days of disappointments and weeks of waiting, world's first successful flight of a self-powered, heavier-than-air flying machine could be possible. The brothers built a movable track to help launch their flying machine, the Flyer to help the aircraft gain enough airspeed to fly. Orville Wright took sustained flight travelling one hundred twenty feet in twelve seconds. Later on November 9, 1904, Wilbur Wright flew his aircraft for more than five minutes for the first time.

In spite of his own disappointment, Langley was thrilled at the success of Wright brothers. He attempted to meet the brothers but they evaded.

Easy to Say

But Press was downright skeptical, not in the least co-operative, forget about any line of encouragement. The Paris edition of the New York Herald wrote in an editorial on February 10th 1906:

"The Wrights have flown or they have not flown. They possess a machine or they do not possess one. They are in fact either fliers or liars. It is difficult to fly. It's easy to say, 'We have flown'."

But the brothers knew they can do it. Every other person warned them that Lilienthal was killed and that Chanute had quit. Still they wanted to fly! They 'could hardly wait to get up in the morning.' Journalists, friends, armed forces specialists, and even their father laughed at the idea of an aeroplane. Wright brothers responded, "We have a dream, and we can make it happen."

First Aeroplane Fatality

Then on September 17th 1908, the disaster dawned upon them. Army lieutenant Thomas Selfridge rode up the plane as an official observer. The flight reached an altitude of about 100 feet (30 m), when a propeller split and shattered. The plane crashed. Selfridge died that evening in the nearby Army hospital with a fractured skull. For the record enthusiasts, that was the first aeroplane crash fatality. Orville suffered a broken left leg and four broken ribs.

A friend visiting Orville in the hospital asked, "Has it got your nerve?"

"Nerve?" repeated Orville, slightly puzzled. "Oh, do you mean will I be afraid to fly again? The only thing I'm afraid of is that I can't get well soon enough to finish those tests next year."

Orville Wright

Soon they were the most famous people in the world, sought after by royalty, rich, and the reporters. The kings and queens came to witness Wilbur fly. At times, tired of explaining the principles of flying, the Wright brothers would say, "The aeroplane stays up because it doesn't have the time to fall."

Neither brother married. They "did not have time for both a wife and an aeroplane." His father Milton wrote about Wilbur in his diary: "A short life, full of consequences. An unfailing intellect, imperturbable temper, great self-reliance and as great modesty, seeing the right clearly, pursuing it steadfastly, he lived and died."

Dream Walk

On Dec. 17th 1903, the first powered flight was made by Wilbur Wright. On July 20, 1969 -- Neil Armstrong becomes the first human to walk on the moon. From the skies in Kitty Hawk to sky-walk in sixty years. That's the power of human endeavour.

Average American boys- they were not rich and famous. Their education was not high and the facilities were not great. But they had an unrelenting desire to succeed,

Average American boys- they were not rich and famous. Their education was not high and the facilities were not great. But they had an unrelenting desire to succeed, their inquisitiveness matching their persistence. In the words of Charles F. Kettering "The Wright brothers flew right through the smoke screen of impossibility."

A young man on the lookout today should fix his goals, examine his strengths, prepare himself, correct his thinking process and face the inevitable failures and discouragements.

You can do it. Do not wait for a fairy or angel pointing out the Road to Success.

Parents often enquire from the more knowledgeable persons where the best opportunities for the future lie.

> ***Our answer is that special opportunities do not exist in the particular industry or profession - they exist within men themselves.***
>
> ***– Kettering***

11 NEVER SAY DIE

These are the words from the scientists who sweated out all their lives to pierce through a dream of an inspiration. We now enjoy the fruits of their toil and turmoil. Many of them lived destitute lives, but one common denominator for successful scientists is "Never say die!" "Never give up!"

Chester Carlson

Take for instance, Chester Carlson, rejected by at least 20 companies including IBM and General Electric. After seven long years of rejections finally a tiny company in New York, the Haloid Company, purchased the rights to his invention, an electrostatic paper-copying machine, which revolutionized offices. Now commonly called Xerox.

Rama Krishna Param Hamsa

But who is this Carlson? He has been granted 34 United States patents, of which 28 relate to xerography. He donated $100 million for various causes before dying of heart attack in 1968. He was a devotee of the Indian sage Ramakrishna, and donated money for the Vedanta Center in Chicago.

Chester F. Carlson was born on February 8th 1906. His father suffered from severe tuberculosis and spent his life lying on the bed due to spinal arthritis. Due to a sick father, poverty and isolation, he was forced to take up work outside school hours at an early age. Still he got his B.Sc. degree in Physics in 1930. He joined the Bell Telephone Labouratories in New York as a Research Engineer. But soon he walked down the streets again, laid off in 1933, during the Great Depression along with thousands of other men.

After repeated trials, he finally landed a job in a patent attorney's office. By 1935, he was more or less settled, but the life was hand to mouth. He received his LL.B. degree in 1939 studying law at night at New York Law School. During the course of his patent work, he dreamt of a small copying machine into which one could feed the original document and get a copy in a few seconds. It is not that there were no copying machines available. They were expensive and unwieldy.

"Nothing happens, but first a dream," Carl Sandburg said. From the basic concept, Carlson refined and re-refined the idea so much that he filed a preliminary patent application on October 18, 1937. Carlson says, "I was charting a new trail and there was no paved highway to the right practical combination."

Disaster Strikes

Then near-disaster struck. Just like his father, he also developed severe arthritis and feared total disability. But Carlson is not one to give up. He was sure to alter adverse conditions to his advantage. He said, "In some ways, this situation also served as an added inducement to produce a marketable invention."

One day in an experiment, sulphur caught fire and filled his home with fumes. Carlson said: "My experiments became very unpopular around the house." Disgusted with his experiments in the kitchen, his wife left him. But his persistence paid off. October 22nd 1938, was an historic occasion as the first photocopy was made with the help of spores of fungus, lycopodium.

Xerox

But soon his trusted assistant left him for greener pastures. Carlson ran from pillar to post with his ideas for seven long years. "Some were indifferent," he said later, "several expressed mild interest, and one or two were antagonistic. The years went by without a serious nibble. I became discouraged and several times decided to drop the idea completely. But each time I returned to try again. I was thoroughly convinced that the invention was too promising to be dormant." Finally, a small company in New York purchased his invention, the photocopying machine. On October 22nd 1948, Haloid Company made the first public announcement of xerography. In 1961, Haloid changed its name to Xerox. That is from where the name Xerox copy comes.

Lonely, tireless and penniless; Carlson defined the pioneering spirit of scientific enquiry, travelling through extreme frustration, failures.

Present generation enjoying high definition televisions with Plasma or liquid crystal displays may not comprehend the travails of television pioneers, or visualize a twelve year old boy, who was described in his school report as "very slow," "timid" and "...by no means a quick learner." He could not even complete his degree in science as World War One broke out and was repeatedly rejected as unfit for army service.

But he had an envious enthusiasm to invent. His career or his home did not leave him much time or money or mental frame, but still he worked relentlessly to overcome these obstacles.

Televisor

Logie Baird was born on August 14th 1888 and his health was never good even as a child. While other children of his age were playing with strings and matchboxes as their toy telephones, he made a telephone exchange and connected his home to four of his friends. Unfortunately one of its low hanging wires caught in an accident and he had to remove his telephone exchange. Never one to waste resources or never one to lose heart, the boy then used these wires to set up a lighting system for his house. He made a homemade glider which threw him with a terrific bump on to the lawn.

In a return trip to Trinidad in 1920, he met an old friend, Captain O. G. Hutchinson by chance who offered help for research. But in late 1922, he became gravely ill and was forced to quit his job. He continued working on his pet television project. Destitute, he became disheveled, shaggy-haired and sallow. His clothes wore thin which he mended with crude patches but continued his thankless research. Can anybody beat Baird in his optimism? Never say die!!

John Logie Baird

By 1924, Baird could make an actual working prototype calling it "Televisor." He mounted a motor on an old tea chest, and attached a homemade Nipkow disc - a cardboard circle cut from a hatbox. A needle became a spindle, and lamp was housed in a discarded biscuit box. It was a precarious contraption, but it worked. How?

While he was racing through his experiments on the transmission of television picture, suddenly there was an image on the screen with unbelievable clarity. Greatly excited, Baird ran to catch hold of the living object, he just saw on the screen. He ran down the flight of stairs, and seized him by the arm. He was his office boy William Taynton. He persuaded him to stay in place and paid two shillings. Baird finally saw a human face recognizably reproduced on his apparatus. Thus, William Taynton became the first TV actor and a professional at that.

Genius is one per cent inspiration and ninety-nine per cent perspiration.

Thomas Alva Edison

12 Only Dead Fish Flows with Stream

Melville De Mellow, one of the greatest news readers of All India Radio once said in an interview, "Only Dead Fish Flows with Stream." The statement had a long impression on me.

Charles Goodyear

This is the saga of man who showed "almost superhuman perseverance" in his search for a stable rubber and in the process developed the vulcanization of rubber. Even though he knew he was drowning, he kept himself alive. He knew he was dying but he swam against the stream. This is not the story of hero of the movies but a true story of the man who brought us vulcanized rubber used in everything from tires, to shoes, and in hundreds of industrial uses.

Goodyear discovered a process to make rubber more stable, and more versatile. Before him rubber was saggy and sticky paste. He was frequently thrown in jail and was scoffed at his invention. When it became successful, it was stolen. The story is saga of failures, and penury.

Charles Goodyear was born in New Haven, Connecticut on December 29th 1800. He was the son of Amasa Goodyear. Charles joined his father's manufacturing business of ivory, metal buttons and agricultural implements. In August, 1824, he married Clarissa Beecher who was a pillar of strength and stood by him through his travails.

In 1818, he opened a hardware store in Philadelphia, though he suffered bad health. Soon the business was on the brink of bankruptcy. But material known as gum elastic, a rubber, caught his eye and he dug out and read every piece of available information on it. He started developing articles with that material.

In the summer of 1834, he met the store manager of Roxbury India Rubber Co., New York, America's first rubber manufacturer with samples. In return the manger showed him racks full of rejected rubber materials. But rubber inspired him. "There is probably no other inert substance, which so excites the mind."

Welcome Jail Gates

As soon as he returned to Philadelphia, jail gates welcomed him. Bad debt!! For Goodyear that was the best place to work. His dutiful wife brought pieces of raw rubber and her rolling pin to the cell. Kneading and rolling for hours and adding bit of magnesia, this or that he produced beautiful pieces of rubber. He thought he got it, end of all his problems.

There are limitless opportunities for us if we only can think and work. For an open mind and willing hand, there are no frontiers. For a great scientist whole universe is labouratory even the jail can be a labouratory.

Soon out of jail, Charles, his wife and small daughters made a number of rubber shoes with that new formula in their kitchen. By summer the shoes turned into shapeless mess. His brother-in-law advised him to feed hungry children first and throw the rubber out. Goodyear replied, "I am the man to bring it back."

'He had a very big idea by the tail, but could he tame it?'(Chester Carlson)

He went on experimenting, making it better, even making decorated models. He developed a method using Nitric acid. A New York businessman advanced thousand dollars for the new development. But the great depression of 1837 took its toll.

He got a government order for 150 mailbags to be manufactured by this new nitric-acid process. Temporary glory soon diminished, the mailbags were a heap of sticky gum. His process failed. His children were back in the backyard digging half-grown potatoes for food.

Leonardo da Vinci said once, "Obstacles cannot crush me. Every obstacle leads to stern resolve. He who is fixed to star does not change his mind." Lonely, tireless and penniless; Goodyear defined the pioneering spirit of scientific enquiry, travelling through extreme frustration and failures.

Vulcanization

In the winter of 1839, Goodyear's endurance paid off; often described as one of the lucky "accidents" resulting in a scientific discovery! There is story that he spilled a mixture of rubber, sulfur and lead onto a hot stove. The hardened mixture was extremely stable and usable. The process was named after Vulcan, the Roman God of fire, as vulcanization, interestingly by a rival.

At last! the breakthrough he had been waiting for! "Nothing happens, but first a dream," Carl Sandburg said. (Carl Sandburg was an American writer and editor who won three Pulitzer Prizes, two for his poetry and another for a biography of Abraham Lincoln.) "Do not wait for your dreams to come true. Work for them in spite of all the odds and abnormalities."

By 1844, he perfected the process sufficiently and pawned everything to make everything like banknotes, musical instruments, almost all household items, and even built pavilions entirely of rubber, floor to roof. He did make rubber crockery, but where is the food?

Once returning from his well-known "hotel" (as he called it), the prison, he found his infant son dead. No money to pay for a funeral, he carried the little coffin to the graveyard. Once he went to New York to meet his daughter only to find her dead.

But he did it, in spite of all the perils and problems. B. C. Forbes says about such scientists, "They won because they refused to become discouraged by defeat!" (Bertie Charles Forbes was a Scottish financial journalist and author. He founded Forbes Magazine, of which he was the Editor-in-Chief until his death in 1954.)

Goodyear is a scientist who swam against the stream, all the way. When he caught the big fish, others stole it from him. He fought with the patent robbers, right up to the U.S. Supreme Court. He made headlines, but not money.

On July 1st 1860, he reached New York to see his dying daughter, only to find that she was already dead. He collapsed and died at the Fifth Avenue Hotel in

New York City. He had $200,000 debt, when he died. However, royalties from his inventions made his family comfortable.

Award in the Jail

Napoleon III awarded the 'Cross of the Legion of Honour' to the scientist. It had to be presented to him in the prison where he was thrown in for non-payment of debts.

His final words, "Life should not be estimated exclusively by the standard of dollars and cents. I am not disposed to complain that I have planted and others have gathered the fruits." We are now enjoying the fruits of his rubber with their myriad varieties and uses in every walk of our lives.

A man has cause for regret only when he sows and no one reaps.

– Charles Goodyear

Let Us Learn to Dream!

Let us learn to dream! said August Kekulé, one of those fascinating figures in the annals of organic chemistry. He discovered tetravalent nature of carbon and structure of benzene rings and interestingly, his insight into these major discoveries came from dreams.

Everyone dreams, but some dreamers realize them to reality. They do when added with an intense passion for invention and innovation. Not all scientific breakthroughs, or good ideas, come through experimentation in the laboratory and there is a place in science for dreamers.

August Kekulé

One afternoon Kekulé was travelling in a bus back to his home at Clapham Road while all his thoughts were on carbon. Sure enough he dropped into an inevitable nap and 'fell into a reverie (a day dream), and lo, the atoms were gamboling before his eyes!' Hitherto, he had never been able to determine the nature of their motion.

But then he saw in his dream, 'frequently, two smaller atoms united to form a pair; how a larger one embraced the two smaller ones; how still larger ones kept hold of three or even four of the smaller; whilst the whole kept whirling in a giddy dance.'

The cry of the conductor: "Clapham Road," awakened him from dreaming; but that night he spent in putting on paper the sketches of the formations from the dream.

"This was the origin of the Structural Theory." He described his dreams thus in a speech given at German Chemical Society. Later, he had another dream where he discovered the structure of Benzene molecule, which was perplexing chemists for a long time.

The meaningful dreams come from much deeper level. They reveal their significance in a poetic form and beauty. The dream in his own description:

He was sitting writing on text book, but the work did not progress as his thoughts were elsewhere. He turned his chair to the fire and dozed. Again the atoms were gamboling before his eyes. He recalled later, "This time the smaller groups kept modestly in the background. Long rows sometimes more closely fitted together all twining and twisting in snake-like motion. But look! What was that? One of the snakes had seized hold of its own tail, and the form whirled mockingly before my eyes. As if by a flash of lightning I awoke; and this time also I spent the rest of the night in working out the consequences of the hypothesis."

The circular structure of Benzene came to Kekulé with visions of the snake seizing its own tail. When Kekule recounted his dream to his colleagues at a scientific convention in 1890, he concluded with the remarks "Let us learn to dream, gentlemen and then we may perhaps find the truth."

Dreams not a Short Cut

Dreams can be a source of inspiration if you are in a creative process. Whether it is a scientist, artist or simple layman, dreams may lead your way to problem solving if you are deeply involved in it. But simple day dreaming will not lend its hand in the scientific or social pursuits. Washington Carver said, "There is no short cut to achievement. Life requires thorough preparation."

But then Kekule was in fact, day-dreaming but deeply involved in what he could not solve. Dreams can make your imagination expand by connecting images, intuition and memories in mysterious ways. Einstein said, "Imagination is more important than knowledge. Knowledge is limited. Imagination encircles the world."

Most of the scientists worked with an imagination coupled with inspiration. They worked under deteriorating economic situation, suspicious governance and hostile environment. They sweated out all their lives to pierce through to a dream of an inspiration. Tireless drive, determination and steadfast optimism kindled by a spark of curiosity led them to the fulfilment of their dreams.

Hand to Mouth Ramanujan

Srinivasa Ramanujan was one of the greatest mathematical geniuses of all time. His leaps of intuition confound mathematicians even today, seven decades after his death. His papers are still probed for their secrets. His theorems are now applied in areas scarcely imaginable during his lifetime. But most of his life was hand to mouth and a hard struggle for existence.

Srinivasa Ramanujan

Ramanujan often said that inspiration for his theorems came in his dreams. His goddess, named Namakkal, would appear in his dreams and present mathematical formulae. He would frequently wake up in the dead of night and work out those formulae on his slate. The sound of his jottings on the stone slates was midnight music for his family members. Slate yes! He even used two slates both sides as he was hard-pressed for hundreds of sheets of paper per day.

Ramanujan described one of his dreams of mathematical discovery thus: "While asleep I had an unusual experience. There was a red screen formed by flowing blood as it were. I was observing it. Suddenly a hand began to write on the screen. I became all attention. That hand wrote a number of results in elliptic integrals. They stuck to my mind. As soon as I woke up, I committed them to writing..."

This mathematical genius said, "An equation means nothing to me unless it expresses a thought of God."

Nowadays, scientists are even trained in methods to increase techniques of dreaming such as dream incubation, dream reentry, and dream recall. These methods will help scientists use their dreaming for creative problem solving.

Many of the modern day products are so interwoven into our lives that we often fail to think of the scenarios, when they were made into reality. Dreams can drive you if you are desperate in the creative process.

Sewing Machine

Take the case of the commonest domestic machine, the sewing machine. For years people wondered if those complicated human motions in stitching can ever be mechanized. Elias Howe also tried his hand in making a sewing machine. He made various combinations of needles, double pointed needles, needles with centre holes, but failed. Then he had a dream where he was taken prisoner by a group of natives. They were dancing around him, their prize catch with spears. There he noticed that all their spears had holes near the tips.

Elias Howe

In some cases solutions are strongly suggested in the dreams. Interpreting dreams can be tricky and only a ready mind can interpret them in the right direction.

As soon as he woke up, he knew that he had a clue to his problem. The hole was located near the tip of the needle and the sewing machine was invented in 1845.

Let us learn to dream, and perhaps then we shall learn the truth. But let us also beware not to publish our dreams until they have been examined by the awakened mind.

– Kekule

That's Nobels all around. And it is family history and upbringing. A Nobel can sense another Nobel. Roger Kornberg once said, "Both my parents had fine scientific minds and taught by example how to approach questions and problems in a logical, dispassionate way. Science was a part of dinner conversation and an activity in the afternoons and on weekends. Scientific reasoning became second nature. Above all, the joy of science became evident to my brothers and me."

Arthur Kornberg

Roger D. Kornberg

Dinner Conversation

Mark the words, *Dinner conversation.* That's the quality time. In the hurry and blurry modern life, parents meet their children only at the dinner time. Take the best out of it. Bring the child's best out. Expand his inquisitive young mind. Develop a sense of purpose and direction in him. Establish the best goals you can. Goals are the seeds of success. So you sow, so you reap!!

It was said,"Arthur Kornberg played a major role in transforming the Stanford University School of Medicine into a research-intensive powerhouse." As a father of remarkably talented children, he nurtured 'a legacy of brilliance and commitment to science and the deepening of our understanding of human life.'

Did Arthur Kornberg imagine that there would be a second Nobel Laureate in the family? "Of course not," he remarked. "But nature is so broad, profound and mysterious — one doesn't know where it leads."

Husband and Wife

In 1947 Carl Ferdinand Cori and his wife Gerty Theresa Cori, née Radnitz shared the Nobel Prize in Physiology or Medicine along with Bernardo Alberto Houssay. Although no one may beat the Curie family's record, there are some more twosome. Gunnar Myrdal received the Swedish central bank's prize for economic sciences in

1974 (considered equivalent to Nobel Prize constituted by The Sveriges Riksbank in Nobel's memeory) and his wife, Alva Myrdal, received the Peace Prize in 1982.

That goes for intelligence, inquisitiveness, stick-it-eveness. Added to them are additional traits -- personality, cognitive capacity, motivation working together. Link them to hereditary patterns and proceed. A hereditary advantage is not sure. But environment, encouragement, inducement do.

Two-in-one

Linus Pauling is the only Nobel Laureate with two unshared awards. He won his first award for his researches into chemical bonds. He also won the Peace Prize in 1962 for his anti-nuclear activism.

Linus Pauling

John Bardeen received the Physics Prize twice: in 1956 for the invention of the transistor and in 1972 for the theory of superconductivity. Frederick Sanger received the prize twice in Chemistry: in 1958 for determining the structure of the insulin molecule and in 1980 for inventing a method of determining base sequences in DNA

Success breeds success.

Facts are the air of scientists. Without them you can never fly.

– Linus Pauling

TEACHER'S PET

In 1946, a boyish-looking man drove a distance of 160 kilometres from Yerkes Observatory in Wisconsin to the University of Chicago. The drive was at least once every week and the objective- only to teach just two students. Why he took so much trouble to teach just two far away students? Why these students wanted this particular teacher? Wait for an explanation.

Subrahamanyan Chandrasekhar

In 1957, these two students, Tsung Dao Lee and Chen Ning Yang were awarded he Noble Prize in Physics. The teacher was Subrahamanyan Chandrasekhar, one of the world's leading astrophysicists. He received a Nobel Prize in Physics from the Swedish King Carl Gustav in 1983 in recognition of his fifty years of work on the structure and evolution of stars.

That's a greater achievement for Dr. Chandrasekhar! His students got Nobel Prize at least 25 years before he got one.

Teachers are in fact the great gardeners. They breed and cultivate generations of inspired minds. Teaching is a profession that teaches all the other professions. It was a teacher who encouraged a young William Perkin to make the first synthetic dye in 1856 and Perkins researches taught another scientist to develop life-saving drugs.

William's father wished him to become an architect, like William's older brother. But the young boy's heart was with chemistry and his talent was easily recognized by his teacher Thomas Hall. One day, when he was fourteen, his teacher advised him to write to Michael Faraday* seeking an invitation to hear the famous scientist's lectures at the Royal Institution. Faraday used to deliver those much-sought-after lectures every Friday at the Royal Institution. Those lectures kindled the spirit in Perkin.

Perkin

Thomas Hall persuaded William's father to enroll him at the Royal College of Chemistry in 1853. One day in 1856, Perkin began to experiment for making synthetic quinine in his home laboratory. His teacher was the inspiration behind these experiments. Instead of a drug for malaria treatment, his experiments ended up in a thick murky mess. But Perkin saw a beautiful purple tint in the mess he created; the colour was brighter and exciting. He just made the first-ever synthetic dye, which didn't fade or wash out and far better than natural dyes. Three years after joining college, he made his discovery, and two years after that, he had made his fortune. He turned twenty then. He left school, opened a factory, and became a millionaire producing the world's first synthetic dye.

After all Alexander the Great said, "I am indebted to my father for living, but to my teacher for living well.

Not the End

Thomas Hall's effort was true to the remarks made by Mark van Doren, "The art of teaching is the art of assisting discovery."

**Michael Faraday did not study much and his education was from the books he used to read as a book binder. And then he was also teacher's pet. Humphrey Davy was asked what his greatest invention was. He replied, "Michael Faraday!"*

But Perkin's discovery is not the end. German bacteriologist Paul Ehrlich was inspired by Perkin's work. He used Perkin's dyes to pioneer immunology and chemotherapy, and made life saving medicines.

All men are born the same. Only teachers make some of them great. "The task of the excellent teacher is to stimulate "apparently ordinary" people to unusual effort. The tough problem is not in identifying winners: it is in making winners out of ordinary people." said Patricia Cross. That was what Dr Alton Ochsner accomplished.

The good teacher makes the poor student good and the good student superior. Dr Alton Ochsner belongs to that class of teachers. He trained about 3,600 talented surgeons including De Bakey. Michael De Bakey was the most famous and highly respected heart surgeons among them.

Michael de Bakey

One day in 1938, Ochsner had opened a patient's rib cage at the Charity Hospital of Louisiana in New Orleans. De Bakey was a trainee assisting him before an assembly of other surgeons. De Bakey pulled back the aorta as precisely as Ochsner had instructed him to do. But that's what the trainee surgeon thought. Actually, he punctured the patient's aorta. Maybe, De Bakey was a bit nervous that his index finger exerted a milligram too much pressure or may be that the patient's tissue weakened.

It was the major artery leading from the heart. De Bakey's heart sank. He thought that he had just killed the patient and he whispered the news to Ochsner.

Ochsner said very calmly to De Bakey's astonishment, "Just leave your finger there. Don't pull it out."

Deftly, Ochsner sutured around the wound in the aorta wall, then said, "Gently now, pull your finger out."

As the trainee heart surgeon pulled his finger out, his young heart began beating normally again. Recalling the incident, De Bakey said afterwards, "Ochsner could, at that moment, have destroyed my confidence and my career. But he did not. He did not curse me, nor embarrass me. He treated it as a simple mistake."

Great Teacher Inspires

In the words of William Arthur Ward, "The mediocre teacher tells. The good teacher explains. The superior teacher demonstrates. The great teacher inspires." Ochsner demonstrated that he was a superior teacher. Often it is remarked that your mother is the Greatest Teacher. She is, no doubt! Here is father who taught the value of learning.

Isaac Asimov is undoubtedly one of the greatest science fiction writers and father of Laws of Robotics.

Looking at so many books in his library carrying wealth of information, his father asked him "How did you learn all this?"

Isaac Asimov

Asimov replied, "From you, Papa!"

"From me? I do not know any of these!"

"You need not have to. You valued learning and taught me to value it. The rest came without trouble."

When you teach your son, you teach your son's son. The Talmud so aspires to become a teacher and inspire minds to explore the universe. Teaching is the noblest profession. While going through the manuscript of this article, one of my students, Anusha read me the following couplet by Sant Kabir. Loosely translated it reads:

"Guru is greater than Govind or GOD (in spiritual form). Guru is the sole person who makes us knowledgeable. Only Guru makes us realize the existence of GOD."

Guru govind dou khare kake lagu paay,
Balihari guru apne govind diyo bataye.

– Sant Kabir

That's Funny

Percy Le Baron Spencer was working on radar technology after WWII in Raytheon laboratory. Magnetrons were manufactured by Raytheon to generate microwaves, which are in the frequencies of a few Giga Hertzs (GHz).

Percy Spencer

He had a candy bar in his pants while he was in the lab one day. Looks like Percy was fond of candies. As he was touring his laboratory, he stood in front of a magnetron. He felt an urge for his chocolate. As he reached for it, he realized that it got melted down. That's funny! His body heat could not have melted the chocolate. Could it be a bad chocolate? His scientific mind prompted him to find out why?

So he experimented. He put an egg near a magnetron and had kept a keen watch on it from a safe distance. As the egg began to tremour and quake, one of his colleagues moved closer to get a better view; the egg exploded and splashed hot yoke all over his face.

But for a minute they were dumbfounded. It is no longer funny. True; rapid raise in internal temperature raised the pressure. How did the temperature rise without any apparent fuel source? Could that be microwaves? Soon it became clear to them that the microwaves are agitating the water molecules in the egg and in the process heating it.

Burnt face or not, they must have laughed themselves off with their discovery. And we have microwave cooking. If only Spencer threw out the molten chocolate from his pant pocket continued with his usual research, microwave cooking would have waited. May be forever.

It will be interesting to note that the first microwave cooker used to weigh about 340kg and 1.67m high and had to be cooled with water.

When the scientists wonder when this funniness required some serious thought, we get some great stuff in our lives. Well, then scientists are not the only ones who stumble across such "funny" things or situations. All of us come across them all the time. But 'we are busy!' We just feel, "that's funny," and walk off to our next urgent task. If Alexander Fleming did not wait to understand and analyze his chance observation...

So next time you see something funny, wait and ponder over it. Ask someone.

That's not Funny

Frenchman, Edward Benedictus, was a jack-of-all-trades. He was a painter, composer, writer and chemist – all rolled into one.

One day a scientific flask slipped off his hands while he was picking it from the top of a shelf. As it crashed on the ground, he hurriedly climbed down the ladder cursing himself. He was amazed to find the flask was broken, but had not actually shattered into pieces. The year was 1903.

That's funny! Why the glass did not break even though it fell from a considerable height. Have the contents in the flask anything to do with it? One of his aides confirmed that the thermos had recently contained cellulose nitrate. Once empty, it was returned to the shelf without proper cleaning.

That's that! The chemical in the flask held the shattered pieces of glass together as an adhesive. We have the safety glass!

Safety glass is now used in windshields for cars, goggles for machinists, and windows and doors for many public buildings wherever shatterproof glass is required. Shattered pieces of glass make some gruesome car accidents. Flying shards of windshield glass make some horrifying injuries. The shreds of glass pierce though the skin and can injure our internals.

Benedictus read a news item that most of the drivers had been injured by shattered glass windshields. He knew that his unique glass could save lives. He wrote in his diary: "Suddenly there appeared before my eyes an image of the broken flask. I leapt up, dashed to my laboratory, and concentrated on the practical possibilities of my idea." For twenty-four hours straight, he experimented with coating glass with liquid plastic, then shattering it.

"By the following evening," he wrote, "I had produced my first piece of Triplex [safety glass]-full of promise for the future." Unfortunately, automakers were not ready to use the costly safety glass for windshields. World War I changed the situation when safety glass found its first practical, wide-scale application as the lenses for gas masks.

His shatterproof glass saved millions in automobile accidents. Think off the situation if he had asked his servant to just clean the floor, throw the broken flask out and walked to his next work.

A number of important discoveries have been made in situations funny or accidental. It takes an extraordinary mind to realize the full potential of an unusual situation and a brilliant brain to build it successfully. Develop both develop your abilities.

Scientific discovery process is not a well understood phenomenon. Great discoveries are results of conscious thought and devoted research of brilliant scientists. Occasionally, they did stumble upon leads which enlightened them on the ultimate object or reality. Funny situations, dreams are only the kindly lights that lead us after the struggle, turmoil, impasse and epiphany.

> ***The most exciting phrase to hear in science, the one that heralds new discoveries, is not 'Eureka!', but 'That's funny...'***
>
> ***–Isaac Asimov***

PARETO PRINCIPLE OR 80-20

As you wake up in the morning, hundred things stare at you waiting to be done. Some of them are "brought forward," some new, taking shape, some look easy, some look difficult and some impossible. Some urgent, some can be postponed, some can be forgotten. Your "FROG" is the one you are most likely to drag your feet on! The "frog" would be the most difficult item in your to-do list, the one you are inclined to postpone. Eat that frog or in other words try finishing that task first. You will be less worried for the rest of the day and will be more confident of attending less strenuous tasks easily. But, if you don't..., the problem, the frog sits in front of you blinking its round eyes. Worst, it will jump on you at the most inopportune moment.

Vilfredo Pareto

So out of ten things, you have in front of you for the day, pick up two most important tasks. These are two tasks which make or break the day. Out of these two, pick the worst one. "If you have to eat two frogs, eat the ugliest one first!" Accomplish that difficult one first. Never attempt to attend the easiest one first. Your ability to select the most important task would be your clinching moment. It will have the greatest positive impact on your life.

Unfortunately, we fail to spot that attending 80% of less useful jobs while the top twenty can yield more results than all of them. Unfortunately, the most useful tasks are most complex and most difficult and we try to procastinate them. But the fruits of those top ten difficult jobs are tremendous. In a list of ten items, two items will be worthier than all others, though they may take same amount of time and effort. In other words 20% rules the 80%. So that's the 80/20 Rule which is one of the most helpful of all concepts of time and life management.

Pareto Principle

The principle was suggested by quality Guru Joseph M. Juran. It was named after the Italian economist Vilfredo Pareto who originally discovered this. Vilfredo Pareto found that 20% of the Italian people owned 80% of that country's wealth. He was born on July 15th 1848 in France and died on August 19th 1923 in Lausanne, Switzerland. He made several important contributions to economics, sociology and moral philosophy, especially in the study of income distribution and analysis. Pareto's social policies were put on paper in his work, Mind and Society.

Pareto observed that Italian society was divided into what he called the "vital few", the top 20 per cent with money and muscle, and the "trivial many", the bottom 80 per cent. He later discovered that virtually all economic activity was subject to this principle as well. But implications of this captivating discovery are far reaching, beyond economics and encompasses every human activity. 80% of your results are explained by 20% of your activities, 80% of your sales come from 20% of your customers, 20% of your products actually result in 80% of your profits, 20% of your tasks will account for 80% of the value, and so on.

Quality Control

Joseph M. Juran (born December 1904 in Romania) is well known as the "father" of quality. He added the human factor to quality, lifting it above raw statistics. Dr. Juran wrote Quality Control Handbook, (1951) and Managerial Breakthrough (1964). In 1979, he founded Juran Institute.

The 80-20 principle is universal. The principle can and should be used by every intelligent person in their daily life.

Joseph M. Juran

In examinations, intelligent students answer the most difficult questions first so that the rest of the answer sheet would be a cakewalk. The students who attempt the easy ones first will soon be running after time. Difficult answers will stare them like a live frog in the plate. Even before the exam, try to understand the most difficult chapter or part of the subject, others will come off easily.

Pareto's theory of predictable imbalance has since been applied to almost every aspect of modern life. Try, it can make a difference. About 20% of your efforts produce 80% of the results. Even in a day-to-day life, you will notice that of all the chores you attend during your day, only 20% really matter. Those 20% produce 80% of your results. Identify and focus on those things. When you look at how much of your profit comes from each item, you will find that 80-20 applies. Put your effort into the 20% that give you 80% of your sales. Similarly, 80% of your sales come from 20% of your customers – the ones who make the big purchases and are repeat-buyers. Cherish that 20%.

Develop the routine of taking up the major task first thing every morning. It is the key to maximize your performance levels. Do not touch the one you can easily accomplish or safely ignore. Terrible waste of time!

Let us start with resume. Understand that the opening lines of your resume must catch the attention of your prospective employers and make them read further. So, in the top 20% of page one, clearly write why you are indispensible. Do not copy the templates available in the computer or on the web. Can't we have some originality? Back up with data or facts and figures and assert yourself. No empty rhetoric! No flamboyant language! No copy and paste! Compel them to read in full. Then there will be 80% chances for your getting a call for an interview.

Pareto in Your Job

Can you guess where 80% of the outcome in the job interview would come from the impression you make in first 1-2 minutes (80% marks if you guessed it right). That is the opportunity waiting for you at the first 20% of the interview time. Make it happen within the first 15-30 seconds. Get the best out of it. It is in your control. People at the other side are professionally rich and past masters in the art. 20% of the opening makes or breaks your job.

That's the Pareto Principle. Use it effectively in your job hunt. The job market is dynamic and constantly changing, it would be impossible to be totally "prepared." But if you had wasted your time hunting the futile 80% in the past, sit up and work back. When you get a job, realize that you are paid and promoted for getting specific, measurable results. This is a world where everything is measured mathematically. Activity is not accomplishment. Measure and manage your results!

These are only few examples of the use you can make of the Pareto Principle. But then the most difficult part of any important job is to begin it. Motivate yourself. Discipline yourself. Overcome procrastination.

Do not misunderstand that by finishing 20% of these more difficult problems, others would automatically solve themselves. No! On the contrary, they will soon become more complicated and critical. So accomplish all the tasks but predict and prioritize.

> ***Eat a live frog every morning, and nothing worse will happen to you the rest of the day.***
>
> ***– Mark Twain***

CHIP OF THE BLOCK

When we listen to the radio or watch television, or travel in train or plane, we have with us culmination of brilliant ideas, collected knowledge, accumulated wisdom and the results of tireless efforts of great scientists.

Jack Kilby

Transistor is an outstanding invention which revolutionized our lives. Remember those good old transistorized radios. But building complex circuits like those in the present day integrated circuits (ICs), which contain millions of transistors and other passive components is sheer 'tyranny of numbers.' Wiring them individually is a mammoth task. It was the scenario when Jack Kilby joined the semiconductor lab at the Texas Instruments.

In that providential July, 1958, he was alone in the deserted labouratory. Kilby wrote, "As a new employee, I had no vacation time coming and was left alone to ponder the results of the IF amplifier exercise... I also realized that, since all of the components could be made of a single material, they could also be made in situ interconnected to form a complete circuit." When he heard this, his boss was enthused but skeptical.

Making the best of his-not-so-vacation-time, the chip was exhibited on September 12th 1958. A sliver of a centimetre wide germanium, narrower than a toothpick, with interconnected wires, on a glass slide! It was shown to the workers, executives and the former chairman of Texas Instruments. When Kilby pressed the switch, "phase-shift oscillator circuit" produced a wave on the oscilloscope. That's the beginning of the first integrated circuit and the world never looked back.

During World War II, the radios used by the military were heavy and unreliable. Kilby travelled to Calcutta for a truckload of black-market radio parts. Soon he built smaller, more reliable radios for the armed forces. That's his attitude, "If something does not meet your requirements, build it!"

Patrick E. Haggerty, former TI chairman, challenged Kilby to design a calculator as powerful as the large, electro-mechanical desktop models of the day, but small enough to fit in a coat pocket. The resulting electronic hand-held calculator, of which Kilby is a co-inventor, successfully commercialized the integrated circuit. While the first IC had only a few components, present integrated circuits and microprocessors contain millions of them. Microelectronics is now the basis of all modern technology, powering everything from household articles, computers to cars to sophisticated machinery, diagnostic equipment, the internet and what not? Jack Kilby was one of the few men whose accomplishments have changed the course of the world.

Interestingly, he 'didn't realize then that the integrated circuit would reduce the cost of electronic functions by a factor of a million to one.' That's the chip, the microchip! And the man: chip of the block or chip off the block?

His younger sister, Jane Kilby recalls, "Our house was full of books...We would recite chunks of Shakespeare at the dinner table, and my parents could finish our sentences if we forgot a passage." The parents Kilbys were graduates of the University of Illinois who encouraged reading. Their house looked like a library. "There were books everywhere," said Jane Kilby. Great chips would definitely come out off such great blocks, when parents spend quality time with children and encourage them in greater life.

But did Jack Kilby take all the credit for this? No! He said "It's true that the original idea was mine, but what you see today is the work of probably tens of thousands of the world's best engineers, all concentrating on improving the product, reducing the cost, things of that sort." Extreme humility of a man who had about 60 patents including a thermal printer!

The demonstration of IC took place in 1958 and he received a Nobel Prize in 2000, more than forty years after his breakthrough. He wrote in his autobiography, "Receiving the Nobel Prize in Physics was a completely unexpected, yet very pleasant surprise. I had to start my pot of coffee very early the morning I received the news that I had been chosen..." Whether the research is applied or basic, we all "stand upon the shoulders of giants," as Isaac Newton said, "I'm grateful to the innovative thinkers who came before me, and I admire the innovators who have followed."

Robert Noyce

Rare breed of humility! He was not unhappy at his late selection to the Nobel "It's not too late - at least I'm still alive. You have to live long enough to receive the Prize," he said.

In a world torn with jealousy, personal egos, pathos and profits, read what Kilby wrote in an autobiography submitted to the Nobel committee, "I would like to mention another right person at the right time, namely Robert Noyce, a contemporary of mine who worked at Fairchild Semiconductor. While Robert and I followed our own paths, we worked hard together to achieve commercial acceptance for integrated circuits. If he were still living, I have no doubt we would have shared this prize." Need we add anything else to speak about the greatness of the man who transformed twentieth century?

While Kilby was developing an integrated circuit with Germanium, Robert Noyce was developing it based on Silicon. In a historical coincidence both invented the IC without knowing each other and about the same time.

In the year 1948, Noyce's girlfriend was pregnant and he needed money for an abortion. His university expelled him for a semester for stealing a pig. To make a living, he took a job at an insurance company. Can you imagine that he later founded Intel with Gordon Moore?

Yes! But he himself said in 1965, "The people that are supervising it (a project) are more dependent on their ability to judge people than they are dependent on their ability to judge the work that is going on."

One day while he was in the college, Robert's physics professor Grant Gale showed them two of the very first transistors coming from Bell Labs. That's the beginning! Noyce was hooked to a lifelong mission of semi conductor development. When he went to MIT in 1948 for his Ph.D., it was accepted that Robert knew more about transistors than most of his professors.

After a brief spell of making transistors for the electronics firm Philco, Noyce decided to work at Shockley Semiconductor. In a single day, he flew with his wife and two kids to California, bought a house, and went to Shockley and asked for a job, well, in that order. But soon Shockley's style of functioning did not fit into Robert's scientific vision. His philosophy, "If you're going to play, play to win!"

Once he won a ping pong game against his father, his mother told him that his father let him win intentionally to encourage him. He was offended. He retorted at his mother, "That's not the game." He was an unbeatably fast learner that his friends called him, "Rapid Robert". The maker of a super intelligent chip!

Seven young disgruntled researchers at the Shockley Semiconductor looked at him as their natural leader. All the eight left Shockley in 1957 and he founded Fairchild Semiconductor in the Silicon Valley long before it earned the name. He was the Sun that rose on the Silicon Valley and he was nicknamed "Mayor of Silicon Valley." At Fairchild he invented the integrated chip and revolutionized the electronics. Chip off the block of silicon! Something more to come from the chip.

Tom Wolfe says in his book 'The Tinkerings of Robert Noyce: How the Sun Rose on the Silicon Valley,' "With his strong face, his athlete's build, and the Gary Cooper manner, Bob Noyce projected what psychologists call the halo effect. People with the halo effect seem to know exactly what they're doing and moreover make you want to admire them for it."

In 1968, he left Fairchild with Gordon Moore (Remember Moore's Law?) to found Intel. At Intel he oversaw Ted Hoff's invention of the microprocessor and revolutionized the industry again. Apart from the chips, he created a work atmosphere at both companies, which has become a standard model of management, where brilliant employees were encouraged to accomplish what they wished. This is often cited as his third revolution.

As the world is becoming flatter and flatter by the revolution in the modern microelectronics, there are the two men behind the inventions of the monolithic integrated circuit - the microchip which laid the technical foundation for it.

In his last interview, Noyce was asked what he would do if he were "emperor" of the United States. His answer was the panacea for the whole world!

> ***...make sure we are preparing our next generation to flourish in a high-tech age. And that means education of the lowest and the poorest, as well as at the graduate school level.***

Robert Noyce

30 What hath God Wrought?

Do you know...

...that Samuel Morse would never have invented the telegraph if the American government had accepted his paintings? Forced to live in poverty with his artistic career, he turned to experimental work in electricity.

Samuel Morse

...that the first telegraph message was transmitted by Morse which read, "What hath God wrought?"

...that Morse used his easel as the armature of the first telegraph apparatus he built?

…that Alfred Nobel was written off as "merchant of death" by newpapers?

…. that while writing his will Nobel did not consult lawyers, "who will prove to you that a straight line is actually crooked?"

…that his fortunes came from war but he fought for peace. He also said, "I intend to leave after my death a large fund for the promotion of the peace idea, but I am skeptical as to its results?"

What has God decided to shape the future? What hath God wrought?

Well! "What hath God wrought?" God decided the beginning of communication revolution. God decided that the merchant of dynamite become the champion of peace. Let be!

Merchant of Death

One day in 1888, an obituary column in news paper headlined "The merchant of death is dead." Further the news item read, "Dr. Alfred Nobel, who became rich by finding ways to kill more people faster than ever before, died yesterday." Alfred Nobel was surprised to read this in the morning paper. The fact was that his brother Ludvig had died. For a moment he sat back and thought, "This is what the future will think of me." He resolved to revise his will. The result? The Nobel Prizes.

When every one of his efforts ended up in unfailing failures, Samuel Morse sent a message that turned out to be the first electronic message ever to be flashed across wires, "What hath God wrought?"

Alfred Nobel was born on 21st October 1833 in Stockholm, Sweden. His father Emmanuel Nobel was an engineer building bridges and buildings. He moved to Russia when his blasting experiments ended up in his bankruptcy. But he returned to Sweden in 1859 as he became bankrupt there also after the Crimean War (1853-56.)

But young Alfred Nobel had the opportunity to work with famous scientists, T. J. Pelouze, and A. Sobrero, an inventor of highly explosive nitroglycerine. Alfred successfully made this liquid explosive, ductile and patented it as dynamite in the year 1867. He also developed a detonator to ignite the explosive with a fuse. Soon this product helped in reducing construction costs and he became one of the wealthiest men in the world.

He experimented with imitation leather, artificial rubber and synthetic silk. He tried to improve the electrical battery, the electric bulb and the phonograph. He was fluent in Swedish, Russian, English, French and German. He built and owned 93 factories around the world, some of which still exist, e.g. Imperial Chemical Industries, UK; Dyno Industries, Norway; and AB Bofors, Sweden. Though described as "the wealthiest vagabond in Europe", he was a workaholic. He said, "my home is where I work and I work everywhere."

But the future generations may read him as the original merchant of death. When he came to know of this, he decided to do something for "the greatest benefit to mankind."

On 27th November 1895, at the Swedish-Norwegian Club in Paris, Nobel signed his last will and testament and set aside the bulk of his estate to establish the Nobel Prizes. The income from the investments was to be "distributed annually in the form of prizes to those who during the preceding year have conferred the greatest benefit on mankind ... the most important discovery or invention within the field of physics; chemical physiology or medicine; literature, the most outstanding work of an idealistic tendency; and one part to the person who shall have done the most or the best work for fraternity between nations. It is my express wish that in awarding the prizes no consideration whatever shall be given to the nationality of the candidates, but that the most worthy shall receive the prize, whether he be a Scandinavian or not."

Most probably, his secretary-cum-house- keeper influenced him to constitute the Nobel Prize for peace, whereas the Nobel Prize for economic sciences was instituted by the Swedish Riksbank since 1968.

Alfred Nobel

Alfred Nobel's estate was spread out in eight European countries and Nobel family was in hot pursuit to grab it. Armed with a gun, Ragnar Sohlman rushed from Paris to St. Petersburg, managed to withdraw all funds and deposit them in a bank vault in Stockholm. But for him, his will would not have been carried out. But then that was what God had wrought?

Alfred Bernhard Nobel died in Italy on 10 December, 1896. The Nobel Prize ceremony takes place on this day.

A man full of paradoxes. Though he was highly successful, yet he felt too little. His fortunes came from war but he fought for peace. Interestingly he said, "I intend to leave after my death a large fund for the promotion of the peace idea, but I am skeptical as to its results." A patriot but spent very little time in his mother land, Sweden. He was not a one-product-wonder. He held as many as 355 patents. Yet he had only one year of formal schooling and no university degree.

It is as, Wilson Greatbatch said, "The Lord was working through me." Greatbatch developed first artificial implantable heart pacemaker. The development came after a mistake he committed while working on an oscillator.

Present generation that got used to and who cannot live without mobile phones and satellite communication, fail to comprehend the troubles and turmoil the scientists underwent who pioneered the products. They invariably looked up to God.

Guglielmo Marconi wrote: "The more I work with the powers of Nature, the more I feel God's benevolence to man; the closer I am to the great truth that everything is dependent on the Eternal Creator and Sustainer; the more I feel that the so-called 'science' I am occupied with is nothing but an expression of the Supreme Will, which aims at bringing people closer to each other in order to help them better understand and improve themselves."

Keep aside wireless which came much later where Marconi was peddled as the inventor of Radio. Let us see what God has written for the wired communication.

Samuel Morse was gifted as an artist. His teaching art at the University of New York left him with a little money. Once after a dinner paid by General Strother of Virginia, he remarked, "This is my first meal for twenty-four hours. Strother, don't be an artist. It means beggary. Your life depends upon people who know nothing of your art and care nothing for you. A house dog lives better..."

Obsession with Electricity

But Samuel Morse was obsessed with the electricity who often heard such classes in college. In 1825, he was commissioned to paint a portrait for $1,000. While he was painting, a horse messenger delivered a letter from his father with one line, "Your dear wife is convalescent". Morse immediately left for his home, leaving unfinished painting. By the time he arrived she had already been buried. Heartbroken for he was not aware of his wife's failing health or her lonely death for days, he thought that he should work for some means of faster communication.

In the autumn of 1832, while travelling home by ship from England, Samuel joined a conversation with some scientific men particularly Dr. Charles Thomas Jackson. That was the turning point for Samuel Morse and the seed for telegraph was sown.

He thought, "If the presence of electricity can be made visible in any part of the circuit, I see no reason why intelligence may not be transmitted instantaneously by electricity."

Morse developed the telegraphic alphabet or Morse Code, and patented it in 1840. It is still the standard application for the coded transmission. After five years of toil, he demonstrated his invention first to his friends and later at Philadelphia's Franklin Institute. He had hoped that someone would buy his invention. But none, not even Congress. Unsuccessfully, he went to England and returned.

He tried another demonstration by under-the-sea cables. Newspapers publicized the event but alas! A ship's anchor caught the wires and experiment ended in a miserable failure. Morse was not a professional engineer or an astute business man. No one believed in him and he was considered a hoax.

First, it is the desire to create to do something original, something no one has ever done. Second the ability to do it. Strong desire acquires ability. Then the quality of persistence, the insatiable desire to keep working, come what may, until it is finished, in spite of the odd surroundings, extreme poverty or terrible health. Next, the dissatisfaction. Though their work looks marvelous to the outside world, they are never satisfied with it. Let us pay tribute to the spirit of these men who have contributed to the conquest of science. Morse belongs to the cadre of such men.

Morse had given up all hope but not his will. What was in store for him nobody knew except God. He applied for a grant and waited on the US Congress proceedings till midnight. Nothing happened. But the next morning Miss Annie G. Ellsworth, daughter of his friend, the Commissioner of Patents brought the news "On the passage of your bill." Morse did not believe her. She then told him that her father sat through until close. In the last moments of the session, the bill was passed without debate with a grant of $30,000 for an experimental telegraph line from Washington, D.C., to Baltimore, Maryland. Morse knew that was his last opportunity.

Just in time Annie Ellsworth handed him the message, which she had chosen from the Bible: "WHAT HATH GOD WROUGHT!" On May 24th 1844, Samuel Morse transmitted this telegraph message from the Supreme Court chamber in the Capitol in Washington, D.C., to the B & O Railroad Depot in Baltimore, Maryland.

Vail forty miles away in Baltimore instantly flashed back the same momentous words, "WHAT HATH GOD WROUGHT!" God willed that the new form of electronic communication begun and develop in an unprecedented pace that every day the communication systems and instruments are getting obsolete yielding place to new.

Wired connection or wireless communication, it would be simply impossible if God thought otherwise. We would have still lived in the caves shouting our signals or sending smoke signs. Nikola Tesla was another great pioneer in electricity and electrical motors, particularly alternating current.

> ***So astounding are the facts in this connection that it would seem as though the Creator, Himself, had electrically designed this planet just for the purpose of enabling us to achieve wonders.***
>
> ***– Nikola Tesla***

Chance Favours the Prepared Mind!

Edison also declared that success comes only after a lot of hard work. Notwithstanding what the scientist with over 1000 patents said, stories are abound with the scientific discoveries made in dreams, by chance and through sheer serendipity. Scientific research itself is based on method, untiring effort. But was it pure chance that made some of the greatest discoveries or is there a Eureka moment?

Benzene-Teflon-Microwave-Apple

The German chemist Friedrich August Kekulé had vision of benzene rings in a daydream.

The wonder material Teflon was invented by Roy Plunkett by accident while trying to develop new gas for refrigeration.

The microwave oven was invented by Percy Spencer; he observed that a candy bar in his pocket had melted when exposed to radar waves.

An apple falling from a tree led Isaac Newton to his theories on gravitation.

Becquerel discovered radioactivity when he mistakenly developed an unexposed photographic film and saw the images of some uranium salts.

Chronicles of these serendipitous discoveries in science fill books. But Louis Pasteur, founder of microbiology and one of the greatest 19th century scientists said, "Chance favours the prepared mind!"

Eureka Moment

If you believe that the "Eureka" moment would arrive, while you are taking a bath, dreaming in a deep sleep or while walking wild side in a park you are mistaken. You are falling in an innovation trap if you sit around waiting for the big idea to hit your brain. Fruitful ideas do not appear in an intellectual emptiness.

The original word, "Eureka" comes from Archimedes who supposedly ran from his bath naked into the streets of Syracuse shouting "Eureka." Probably Archimedes never uttered the word. This oft repeated story started with Vitruvius, a Roman writer, in the first century B.C.

As the story goes…

Hieron II, the King of Syracuse engaged a craftsman with a certain amount of gold to be crafted into a beautiful crown. Exquisite it was, the king soon started wondering whether the crown was all of pure gold he gave the goldsmith or had he been cheated. King summoned Archimedes to find out without even making a scratch on it.

Why Archimedes?

Archimedes is revered even now as a mathematical genius. With his mastery over engineering and physics, he is claimed to have said, "Give me a place to stand on and I can move the world."

He worked on the basic mechanics of lever. Make a long lever; fix it to a centre with a short end on the other side. Any weight could be lifted at the short end. If only you could stand somewhere…

King Hiero thought that the scientist was a bluff. So Archimedes chose a ship at the dock fully loaded with freight and passengers. He tied the ropes in pulleys and levers arrangement. Pulling the ropes, single-handedly, he drew the ship slowly into the sea.

That was when the king developed him the confidence and entrusted him with the gold crown. The king even issued a proclamation stating: "…Archimedes is to be believed in everything that he may say."

Archimedes was born at Syracuse, Sicily around 287 B.C., son of an astronomer and related to Hiero II, who ruled Syracuse from 270 to 216 B.C. Sicily was then a Greek land. He studied at Alexandria, Egypt, the intellectual centre of the Mediterranean world. He was ashamed of his interest in mechanical devices, but kept on making them. Archimedes did what no man before him had done: he applied science to practical problems of everyday life. Today his fame rests upon them.

A for Archimedes

Archimedes principles, Archimedes screw, Archimedes levers. Eureka!! They are part of mankind's heritage. That makes him unique forever.

Back to the story. Deeply immersed in his thoughts of solving the problem, (in the modern parlance, "Non-destructive testing"), he stepped into a bathing pool.

Anyone can observe that water just spills over as you step into a full bathing tub. Only a prepared mind could foresee a solution to a problem. As the water splashed out, delighted that he has the answer for the crown, he leapt out of the pool into the streets, naked, cried aloud in Greek: Eureka! Eureka! ("I have found it"). He realized that the volume of an irregular object could be measured by measuring the volume of the water it displaces. He had a prepared mind and working for it even while bathing.

Chris Rorres, a mathematician at the University of Pennsylvania remarks, "The eureka moment was maybe due to his original discovery [concerning buoyancy], not to sitting in the bathtub and then running through the streets of Syracuse naked."

Afterwards he took a piece of pure gold and another of pure silver with weights equivalent to that of the crown. He immersed all three of them, in water successively and measured the volume of water that overflowed with each material. Archimedes uncovered a fraud using his principle of buoyancy. All the vessels that sail on or under water are governed by the principle of buoyancy of Archimedes.

So, don't wait for the big idea to hit you. Just get started innovating and never stop. Most of us hit mysteries often, but we simply ignore them. But scientists stop, wonder and ponder over them. We enjoy the fruits of those tireless efforts. Skills marking out a Prepared Mind are observation, learning, imagination, reasoning, challenge and reflection. In a constantly changing world, observe and learn. Past knowledge brought you here. Update knowledge in your main focus areas. Reasoning had been a primary tool in the scientific research. So discern the conforming, non-conforming and disconfirming information.

Einstein said, "Imagination is more important than knowledge," and "Knowledge is limited; but imagination encircles the world". Latest branch of engineering getting ground is Imagineering or idea engineering. And then scientific breakthroughs are made by challenging old notions and dogmas.

Reflect on your ideas. New ideas may not right away succeed. Nineteenth century theories and formulae, which were almost buried deep, are now put into some of the most effective uses now with the advent of modern technological developments.

Innovation is far more about incremental and improvement than about the "Eureka" moment. Lewis Thomas, renowned science author and former president of Memorial Sloan-Kettering Cancer Center stated, "I'm not as fond of the notion of serendipity as I used to be... You create the lucky accidents."

Let us consider another accident, lucky or not?

In 1945, Nobel committee awarded three men, Alexander Fleming, Ernst Chain and Howard Florey the Nobel Prize in physiology or medicine for the discovery and isolation of penicillin. Most textbooks credit a chance observation, made in 1928 by Fleming alone, for the discovery of penicillin.

Fleming actively researched for anti-bacterial agents, particularly for a chemical that can heal the wounds caused by bullets. In the process, he discovered lysozyme, an enzyme found in body fluids such as tears, which has a natural antibacterial effect, though mild.

On a momentous day in 1928, he was looking at a pile of Petri dishes where he had been growing bacteria. Fleming opened each dish and examined it before dropping it for cleaning. In one dish he noticed a patch of "blue mould" (like the one on spoiled food). Funnily there were no microbes immediately around this mould. After some testing, Fleming concluded that the mould stopped the growth of those particular bacteria. He tested it on lab animals and found its anti-bacterial qualities. He named it penicillin.

He created a lucky accident. Fleming's discovery could have been nothing but a stroke of luck but for the base knowledge provided, by the observations of Roberts, Pasteur, Lister, Joubert and others. Thus the stage was set for the "chance" discovery of penicillin by Alexander Fleming in 1928. Despite this success, Fleming failed to produce a concentrated extract of penicillin.

In 1939, Ernst Chain, Howard Florey and Edward Abraham of Oxford University were able to purify and produce penicillin. The first demonstrated trial was on a policeman in 1941. The patient recovered but died. Penicillin was so scarce that excreted penicillin from the patient's urine was collected and recrystallized for reuse. The therapeutic efficacy of penicillin was accepted. At the onset of World War II, war cries demanded more of this wonder drug.

In a courageous act, Ernst Chain sailed across the war torn Atlantic to the United States for its mass production. Penicillin saved thousands of lives in the World War II and afterwards. Florey and Chain transformed a labouratory curiosity into a practical drug.

> ***Opportunity often goes unrecognized because it usually goes around wearing overalls and looks a LOT like hard work. I never did anything worth doing by accident; nor did any of my inventions come by accident; they came by work.***
>
> ***– Thomas Edison***

UNIQUE YOU

As soon as you enter the room in the evening, you switch on the light. Immediately, a few of us think of the inventor Thomas Alva Edison. Many of others may not think of any one. We just take for granted the light falling on us. On sweaty day, we switch on a fan. Who was behind this invention? Nikola Tesla! While relaxing on the sofa, you switch on the television. Whole range of entertainment dances before you. Whose effort was that? Logie Baird and Farnsworth! Then the telephone rings. We answer the phone even without thinking of Alexander Graham Bell.

For many of us sea travel is an experience or a voyage or a business trip, for CV Raman it was scientific expedition. The result was Raman Effect and Nobel Prize. A painter's sea voyage heralded communication explosion for us. Samuel Morse! Remember his dot-dash- dot! The Morse code! Communication technology may have taken leaps and bounds but his Morse code stays! The original electric bulb invented by Edison is slowly getting obsolete with the advent of florescent and LED bulbs. But Edison still stands tall.

It is a common place now but in all the childhood curiosity, we used to run to the open courtyard to watch an aeroplane going high above our house. But skeptics said that "objects heavier than air can be flown." Wright Brothers proved them wrong.

Those are the creative minds whose unrelenting efforts resulted in numerous inventions and discoveries that constantly change the course of our lives. Those are the inspired brains or ignited minds that lead to inventions and discoveries.

Abdul Kalam asks, "Are you willing to become a unique personality?"

He answers from his own experience, while he met about 11 million youth in India and abroad, in a decade's time. He says, "every youth wants to be unique, that is, YOU! But the world all around you, is doing its best, day and night, to make you just "everybody else".

Then if you want to become one, unique you, you can become one.

One Man Army, Ever

We often talk about ONE MAN ARMY. Wars are no longer fought with arrows and spears. Now with Guided missiles and misguided men! Whether the wars are fought with arrows or atom bombs, there was only one man army, ever, ever.

The strongest army in the ancient world was Rome. An old man over seventy, held the Roman army to a standstill for nearly three years and almost won. He set up curved mirrors on the walls of Syracuse, and burnt Roman ships. No Lasers, no secret software, no complicated guidance systems. The old man was Archimedes of Syracuse, the greatest scientist of the ancient world. He built long arms and huge claws which caught the ships and overturned them. No hydraulics but pure mechanics. It was Archimedes.

Archimedes held off the Roman army for three years. When in 212 BC Syracuse surrendered to Rome, Marcellus, the Roman King told his men, "Spare that mathematician". That's unique! A soldier ordered him to surrender, not knowing who he was. Archimedes paid no attention as even defeat could not affect his restless brain. "Don't disturb my circles," said Archimedes. That's unique! The enraged soldier killed him.

And he, exclusive!! And unique you? Where are you?

If you want to take the challenge and become "unique you", 'you have to fight the hardest battle, which any human being can ever imagine to fight; and never stop fighting until you arrive at your destined place, that is, a UNIQUE YOU!' Are you ready for a fight? Do you want to be a Unique You or Everybody else?

Archimedes discovered some of the most fundamental principles in science, from a practical problem of adulteration of gold. He turned abstract theories in science to everyday solutions to mechanical engineering problems. That's what is unique about 'A for Archimedes.' If you want become some special, he is the last word.

Only One Marconi

Marconi was commissioned by the queen to install a wireless network from the Royal yacht to her summer residence in the Isle of Wight. Her son (who later became Edward VII) was recovering from a leg injury on the Royal Yacht.

Once while walking in the garden, the queen ignored to return his greetings. In huff he decided to relinquish the job.

The queen immediately ordered to get another electrician.

The queen was politely told, "This world is full of electrical wizards. But there is only one Marconi."

Marconi

Marconi was my role model, so also Edison. Until I read about Jagadish Chandra Bose and Nikola Tesla.

Is there another scientist at home in his biological researches as well as investigations in physics?

Sage Reborn

May 1901, London. That great scientist was giving finishing touches to a lecture to be delivered in the Royal Society. An unusual glow was radiating from his face, as if he is an Indian sage reborn. A call disturbed his deep concentration and it was a telegram. He looked at it in disbelief as an industrialist was requesting for an urgent meeting with him. The scientist had no time on hand to meet even a multimillionaire. He sent a reply immediately with a firm 'No!' Soon another telegram arrived informing him that he was coming down himself.

As the scientist was about to leave for the lecture, there came, Major Stephen Flood Page, the Managing Director of the Marconi's Wireless and Telegraph Company.

"He made an earnest request not to divulge all valuable research results in today's lecture: 'There is money in it -- let me take out patent for you. You do not know what money you are throwing away… I will only take half share in the profit – I will finance it,' etc., etc." This multimillionaire was 'pleading like a beggar.' The scientist refused and delivered his lecture at the Royal Society.

Jagadish Chandra Bose

That was Jagadish Chandra Bose in a letter on 17-05-1901 to Rabindranath Tagore, his lifelong friend. He also wrote, "I once get sucked into this terrible trap, there won't be any escape! See, the research that I have been dedicated to doing, is above commercial profits." He had the qualities of saintly selflessness, like plants and trees, whose intricate secrets he unraveled.

Dr. Muirhead of Muirhead & Co requested Bose 'to keep his inventions a secret.' But he was an Indian sage reborn!! He had philosophical revulsion for greed and refused to patent his findings.

But his love for biology never diminished. May 9, 1901, the hall of the Royal Society in London was packed with eminent scientists, royal men and women. Bose wanted to show that plants have feelings and suffer pain. A highly sensitive and delicate instrument relayed the pulse of the plant on to a light spot on a screen indicating it in a vibrant movement like the pendulum of a clock. Now Bose dipped the plant down to its stem in a vessel containing bromide poison and started watching, as everyone else, expectantly at the light spot to diminish and die.

But alas! No! Its pulse was steady. The scholarly spectators started laughing. With his characteristic calmness, he examined the poison bottle and took to his mouth. Depressed? Ashamed? No, but with utmost confidence! If it was real poison, his experiment should work. If not, it can't kill him also. At that very moment a man in the audience stopped him short and shouted that he had put similar coloured water in the poison bottle. Some of the jealous scientists paid him to sabotage the experiment, well almost!

Next day, Bose conducted the experiment again with thundering success. He said, "If there had been any success in my life that was built on the unshakable foundation of failure…" Soon the light became wobbly, began vibrating fiercely indicating a violent death of the plant. The scientist received a standing ovation from the distinguished audience. Bose almost took the poison himself to prove his experiment right. Like legendary Karna, his childhood idol, he had the courage to fight against odds. That places him in a unique position not only among Indian scientists.

Bose, Tesla, Carver belong to this cadre as quoted in "A Visit to Nikola Tesla" by Dragislav L. Petković in Politika ; also in Tesla, Master of Lightning (1999) by Margaret Cheney, Robert Uth, and Jim Glenn.

"Money does not represent such a value as men have placed upon it. All my money has been invested into experiments with which I have made new discoveries enabling mankind to have a little easier life. "

No Alternate

Here are the prophetic words from a scientist before the advent of twentieth century.

"Within a few years, a simple and inexpensive device, readily carried about, will enable one to receive on land or sea the principal news, to hear a speech, a lecture, a song or play of a musical instrument, conveyed from any other region of the globe." We now know that simple inexpensive device is the mobile phone. And the man who said this was not a science fiction writer but a prolific inventor who saw the world far ahead of others. He brought us an invention that changed the face of the globe forever. This was the invention of the induction motor. Think of him for a moment when the power fails. He invented and brought alternating current to our homes.

Nikola Tesla

When this 6'4" immigrant from Eastern Europe entered Thomas Alva Edison's office, he was thrilled. He handed over his letter of recommendation to Edison with certain amount of trepidation. It read: "My Dear Edison, I know two great men and you are one of them. The other is this young man!" That other man was Nikola Tesla. That's unique about him and he proved it to the hilt.

He was scientist, poet and a visionary who could look beyond centuries. His inventions 'created a sensation such as no other invention has ever produced.'

While presenting Tesla with the Edison medal, Vice President Behrend of the Institute of Electrical Engineers spoke the final words: "Were we to seize and eliminate from our industrial world the result of Mr. Tesla's work, the wheels of industry would cease to turn, our electric cars and trains would stop, our towns would be dark and our mills would be idle and dead. His name marks an epoch in the advance of electrical science."

Mr. Behrend ended his speech with a change in the original Pope's lines on Newton:

Nature and nature's laws lay hid by night.
God said 'Let Tesla be' and all was light.

So do you want to be unique or just another one in this planet of billions? In his speech at Dayalbagh Educational Institute (Deemed University) Kalam asks,

"Will you be remembered for a visionary action for the nation, like Mahatma Gandhi, Pandit Nehru and Sir C.V. Raman?

Will you be remembered for creating a company which finds a place in the top 100 of the Fortune 500 companies from India?

Will you be remembered for developing one million enlightened youth in your region who will participate in the accelerated societal transformation of the state and the nation?"

Don't keep forever on the public road, going only where others have gone. Leave the beaten track occasionally and dive into the woods. You will be certain to find something you have never seen before. It will be a little thing, but do not ignore it. Follow it up, explore all around it; one discovery will lead to another, and before you know it, you will have something worth thinking about.

– Alexander Graham Bell

NEVER GIVE UP

When we walk into a room and put on the light switch, only a rare few of us think of the inventor Edison. But those even those who think of him would smile in disbelief to know that once electric light was considered impossible.

Thomas Alva Edison

The New York Times published an article on January 16th 1880. "After a few more flashes in the pan, we shall hear very little more of Edison or his electric lamp. Every claim he makes has been tested and proved impracticable."

No wonder in The New York Times' claims; Edison and his assistants tested more than 6000 materials as a right material for the filament. He tried over 2000 experiments and over 13 months before he got the light bulb to work.

At some point in life we feel like giving up, particularly after repeated failures. The lowest class people do not even start for fear of losing. Middle class people leave it half way down when they face obstacles; a time when most of us turn back and withdraw from the scene. But greatest are those who pursue till the end in spite of repeated failures and insurmountable obstacles. Histories are written on their lives. Success comes to those who endure the falls. It comes to those who have the courage to get up after every one of the falls, time and again.

If you are looking for inspiration, think of Edison, Goddard and Tesla. Let nothing stop you from achieving success. Never give up when you feel utterly lost and depressed. Sometimes we give up just before we are about to make that huge breakthrough for which we have been putting so much effort to achieve.

In a final attempt, Mr. Batchelor, Edison's assistant held his breath and carried a tiny thread bent into the shape of a horseshoe as they were going to a glass blower's house. They had to insert this in a glass bulb, seal and create vacuum. "Just as they reached the glass blower's house, the wretched carbon broke." This was a moment of the greatest dilemma. Give up or not?

Edison thought, "Our greatest weakness lies in giving up. The most certain way to succeed is always to try just one more time." Give up only when you are dead.

They turned back and produced another carbon, which was also broken by a jeweler's screwdriver falling on it. By nightfall another carbon was made and inserted. The bulb was exhausted of air and sealed. Finally at 1:30 a.m., the current turned on, and the bulb was lit which glowed for an unexpected 10 ½ hours.

You cannot master everything right away. Learning takes time and you are bound to make mistakes. Learn from them. The next story is often recounted in motivational lectures. A young reporter asked him how it felt like failing so many times. He said, "I never failed once. I invented the light bulb. It just happened to be a 2000-step process." Many laughed and some sympathized with him. In reply to a friend, Edison said, "I discovered hundreds of materials that do not make filament. The electric light has caused me the greatest amount of study and has required the most elabourate experiments." As long as you are alive and kicking, keep trying until you succeed. Continue to walk on the darkened alleys, see the end of the night and see the light of the day.

So Edison did not stop there and the next trial was with a carbonized sewing thread which lasted unprecedented 45 hours. Edison records: "None of us could go to bed, and there was no sleep for any of us for 40 hours. We sat and watched it with anxiety growing into elation. The lamp lasted about 45 hours, and I realized that the practical incandescent lamp had been born." Do not sleep when the light at the end of the tunnel is about to shine.

There will always be haters, who will discourage you and even try to pull you down. Do not care for them or get carried away by them but carry on with your idea. Edison believed in himself and turned a deaf ear to others. For instance, a British Parliamentary Committee was assigned to investigate the value of an electric bulb. Its report on the invention says, "Good enough for our transatlantic friends…. But unworthy of the attention of practical or scientific men."

Let them talk, let them pull you down. Let them throw unsolicited and saintly advice. Never give up until you reach your goal! You deserve success.

> ***Keep on going, and the chances are that you will stumble on something, perhaps when you are least expecting it. I never heard of anyone ever stumbling on something sitting down.***
>
> ***– Charles F. Kettering***